A Hit - man's Kill - er

Written by: Willie S.

Preface

Jack Nubold graduated with honors and a mountain of debt. Medicine had been his compass; necessity became his detour. When the bills proved louder than the oath, he answered a different call—one that paid in cash and silence.

He found his first contract through friendly connections, a name that fit the ledger: **David Fordes**. Jack watched, learned habits, and chose a night when rain would wash footprints and dull the world's attention. Breaking into a dim living room, he expected a struggle; instead he found a body slumped on a couch, an overdose already done. He finished what the world had begun with a single, clinical shot to the head.

The payout was **one million dollars**—enough to clear tuition, loans, and the future he thought he'd bought. The morning news reported a gunshot death and Jack slipped back into anonymity. Two months later the coroner's report changed the story: David had been dead before the bullet. The headline that followed was a different kind of verdict.

Now the ledger has been reopened. A price has been put on Jack's head to reclaim the money he took. He runs with the knowledge that the rules of his new trade are ironclad: **never break the hitman's code**. What began as a desperate transaction to settle debts has become a flight through shadows, where every choice is surgical and every ally might be a ledger entry in someone else's account.

Table of Contents

Chapter 1: All the Bills Add Up

Jack Nubold had spent the last eight years of his life learning how to keep people alive, or at least how to convince them that a defibrillator and a soothing bedside manner could do the trick. He had memorized Latin terms that sounded like exotic pasta, performed procedures that required both steady hands and a tolerance for bad coffee, and survived a residency that taught him the true meaning of the phrase **"sleep is optional."** He had also, as of last Tuesday, graduated. The diploma was framed, the mortarboard was ceremonially tossed, and the family photos were already doing their best to make him look like a responsible adult.

Then he opened the envelope marked **"Itemized Account Statement"** and discovered that adulthood had a punchline and it was printed in twelve-point Times New Roman. The bills were not so much a stack as a geological formation: tuition, fees, interest, mysterious charges labeled "administrative convenience," and one line item that simply read **"You Owe Us Everything."** Jack sat at his kitchen table, which had seen better days and fewer unpaid utilities, and tried to decide whether to cry, faint dramatically, or invent a new medical specialty that paid in cash.

He tried the usual options. He considered becoming a medical influencer, which involved filming himself applying bandages while offering life advice in between sponsored segments for herbal toothpaste. He briefly entertained the idea of opening a boutique clinic for people who wanted their ailments diagnosed with artisanal empathy. He even Googled "how to monetize a stethoscope" and learned that the internet had opinions and very few solutions.

Then, like a badly timed flashback in a sitcom, he remembered a conversation from third year. Over stale cafeteria pizza and a mutual disdain for morning rounds, his friend Marco had mentioned, in a tone that suggested he was describing a weekend hobby rather than a career choice, that he "knew people who did discreet work." Marco had said it with the same casualness he used to recommend a good cardiology textbook. Jack had laughed then, because the idea of a med student moonlighting as a hitman felt like a punchline in a bad noir parody. Now, staring at the bill that could fund a small country, the laugh lodged somewhere between his throat and his sense of fiscal responsibility.

Jack called Marco.

Marco answered on the third ring, as if he had been waiting for this exact moment and had been practicing his nonchalance in the mirror. "Jacko! How's the world's newest doctor?" he asked, which was Marco's way of saying hello and also reminding Jack that he had once been a person who could afford coffee.

Jack explained the situation with the economy in the tone of someone reading a weather report about a hurricane. Marco listened, and then, with the solemnity of a man who had once recommended a particularly effective brand of duct tape, said, "You know, there are people who can help. Not the kind of help with pamphlets and empathy. The kind of help with cash."

Jack's brain, trained to diagnose and triage, tried to run a differential. Option A: Marco was joking. Option B: Marco was not joking and had a very specific set of acquaintances. Option C: Jack had accidentally wandered into a late-night infomercial for questionable life choices. He chose Option B because his bank account had already chosen bankruptcy.

Marco invited him to meet someone "who could explain things." The meeting was scheduled at a coffee shop that smelled faintly of burnt ambition and espresso. The person who explained things was named Lester, which is the sort of name that belongs on a man who wears sunglasses indoors and has a business card that says nothing but a phone number and the word **"Solutions."** Lester's handshake was firm, his smile practiced, and his résumé suspiciously blank.

Lester did not, to Jack's relief, hand him a manual titled *How to Be a Professional Problem Solver in Ten Easy Steps.* He did, however, hand him a brochure that looked like it had been photocopied from a 1990s self-help seminar. The brochure used words like "discreet," "efficient," and "no questions asked," which, in the context of a man who had once sutured a patient's eyebrow back into place, sounded both terrifying and oddly practical.

"What's the catch?" Jack asked, because he had been trained to ask that question before prescribing anything.

"No catch," Lester said, which was the sort of answer that made Jack's medical instincts tingle. "Just a code. Rules. Professionalism."

Jack, who had once sworn an oath to do no harm and then promptly learned that the world interpreted oaths as suggestions, found himself bargaining with ethics like a man haggling at a flea market. He told himself he would be surgical about it—metaphorically surgical, because the literal kind was still his day job in theory—and that he would only take on work that didn't involve moral ambiguity thicker than the hospital's cafeteria gravy.

Lester explained the logistics in a way that was intentionally vague and suspiciously efficient. There were contacts, intermediaries, and a payment structure that involved envelopes and a level of secrecy that made Jack nostalgic for the days when his biggest secret was a failed anatomy exam. The money, Lester said, was real. The risks, Lester said, were manageable if one followed the rules. The rules, Lester said, were simple: **never break the code.**

Jack left the coffee shop with a business card that had no name and a head full of rationalizations. He rationalized like a surgeon prepping for a risky operation: methodically, with a checklist and a steady hand. He told himself he would only do what was necessary to clear his debts, that he would never enjoy it, and that he would retire from this side hustle the moment his student loans were a memory. He also told himself he would never, under any circumstances, become the sort of person who used phrases like "side hustle" in a sentence that also included "moral compromise."

Back at his apartment, Jack spread his bills across the table like a forensic investigator examining the scene of a financial crime. He did the math, which in his case involved a calculator, a lot of sighing, and the occasional muttered curse at compound interest. The numbers were stubborn and unhelpful. The million-dollar fantasy that had seemed like a punchline in a noir film suddenly looked like a very specific solution.

He imagined, briefly and with the kind of detachment that comes from reading too many case studies, what it would be like to hand over the last of his debt in a single envelope. He imagined the relief, the freedom, the ability to sleep without dreaming of overdue notices. He also imagined the absurdity of explaining to his mother that he had paid off his loans through "discreet financial arrangements," and decided that some conversations were best avoided.

So Jack took a breath, put on his most neutral face, and called the number on the nameless card. The voice on the other end was calm, efficient, and disturbingly cheerful. "We'll find a way," it said. "We'll make it clean."

Jack, who had spent years learning how to stitch people back together, realized he was about to stitch his life into a new pattern—one that involved envelopes, codes, and a very specific kind of discretion. He told himself it was temporary. He told himself he would be careful. He told himself he would never, ever use the phrase "professional discretion" in casual conversation.

As he hung up, a pigeon landed on his windowsill and looked at him with the kind of judgment only birds and unpaid creditors can muster. Jack smiled at the pigeon, because humor was a defense mechanism and also because the alternative was to panic. He had chosen a path that was absurd, dangerous, and possibly illegal, but it was also, in a way that made his stomach do a small, nervous flip, the most practical option he had.

He made a list. The list had three items: **1. Pay bills. 2. Keep hands clean. 3. Never break the code.** He underlined the third item twice, because rules were easier to follow when they were written in ink and not in the shaky handwriting of desperation.

And so, with a diploma on the wall, a mountain of debt on the table, and a pigeon as an unwilling witness, Jack

Nubold stepped onto a path that promised cash, secrecy, and a new set of ethical dilemmas. It was not the career he had imagined when he first dreamed of medicine, but then again, life rarely follows the script you studied in school. It tends to improvise, and Jack was about to learn the comedic timing of improvisation the hard way.

Chapter 2: Into Cool Water

Jack had always imagined his first official day in the "real world" would involve a white coat, a stethoscope, and at least one awkward handshake with a hospital administrator who smelled faintly of peppermint and regret. He had not pictured fluorescent office lights, a potted plant that looked like it had given up, and a receptionist who wore sunglasses indoors and a nameplate that read **Jahlain** as if it were a single-word prophecy.

He found the office on the south side, which in guidebooks is usually described as "eclectic" and in reality means "lots of parking meters and a suspiciously high number of locksmiths." The building lobby had the kind of carpet that had seen three decades of spilled coffee and one ill-advised office party. Jack rehearsed his face in the mirrored elevator—neutral, competent, not like someone who had once considered paying off student loans by selling artisanal bandage kits on Etsy. He practiced his handshake in his head and decided that whatever handshake he used, it should not involve a pulse check.

The receptionist's desk was a shrine to efficiency and passive-aggression. There were pens chained to the counter, a bowl of mints that had been there since the Clinton administration, and a small plaque that read **"No Drama."** Jahlain sat behind it like a monarch who had chosen bureaucracy as a throne. She wore a blazer that suggested she had once been a spy in a previous life and now specialized in filing forms with the same intensity.

"Name?" she asked, not looking up from a spreadsheet that could have been used to calculate the trajectory of a falling soufflé.

"Jack Nubold," he said, which sounded less like an introduction and more like a diagnosis.

Jahlain finally looked up, and the world tilted slightly because she had the kind of expression that could make a tax auditor feel judged. "Doctor Nubold," she said, as if testing the syllables for authenticity. "You're early. That's either very responsible or very suspicious."

"Responsible," Jack lied, which was his default answer for everything from parking tickets to life choices that involved moral ambiguity.

She handed him a clipboard with the kind of efficiency that suggested she had once been a drill sergeant in a past life and had been demoted to administrative overlord for being too punctual. The form asked for the usual—name, contact, preferred pronouns—and then a line that read **"Experience Level"** with options: *Novice, Competent, Professional, Mythical.* Jack circled **Novice** with the solemnity of a man admitting he'd once failed a pop quiz on ethics.

"You trained?" Jahlain asked, eyebrow doing a thing that implied she had seen many people try to bluff their way through life.

"Sort of," Jack said. "My dad took me to shooting ranges when I was a teen. Retired military. Taught me the basics. Mostly about patience and not losing your temper when the target is a paper silhouette that looks suspiciously like your ex."

Jahlain made a sound that could have been sympathy or a suppressed laugh. "Basics are fine. We don't hand out nuclear codes on the first day. We hand out small, manageable problems and a lot of paperwork."

Jack tried to imagine paperwork as a weapon. It did not help.

She led him down a corridor that smelled faintly of lemon cleaner and unresolved decisions. The office décor was a tasteful blend of "we have money" and "we prefer not to advertise it." There were framed certificates on the wall that said things like **"Discretion: Level 3"** and **"Conflict Resolution: Advanced"**—phrases that made Jack feel like he had accidentally wandered into a very niche continuing education seminar.

"First assignment," Jahlain said, sliding a manila envelope across the desk like it was a casserole dish at a potluck. "Novice level. Low complexity. High reward."

Jack's heart did a small, medically concerning flip. He had been trained to read charts, not envelopes. He opened it with the same reverence he'd once reserved for anatomy textbooks and found a single sheet with a name on it: **David Fordes**.

"David Fordes," Jahlain repeated, as if tasting the syllables. "He did business that went south. Stole from the wrong people. Hides out. Drinks like a man trying to forget his own name. Drugs. Bad ticker. Not exactly a poster child for longevity."

Jack read the description and felt a strange mix of professional curiosity and the kind of moral queasiness that comes from realizing your résumé now includes "discreet problem solver." He pictured David as a tragic figure in a noir film—cigarette smoke, a fedora, a heart monitor flatlining dramatically. Instead, Jahlain's description painted him as a man who had made a series of poor life choices and then doubled down with a loyalty to bad decisions.

"Is he dangerous?" Jack asked, because that was the question his training had taught him to ask first.

"Dangerous?" Jahlain echoed. "Not in the way that requires tactical reinforcements. Dangerous in the way that a leaking roof is dangerous—eventually it ruins everything if you ignore it. He's slippery, but mostly because he's greasy from too many late-night takeout orders and questionable life choices."

Jack tried to imagine approaching a greasy, heart-troubled man and felt his stomach do a small, nervous somersault. He had been a novice at suturing and a novice at sleep deprivation; he was now a novice at moral compromise. He thought of his father's lessons at the range—patience, breath control, respect for the tool—and tried to translate them into something that didn't involve a lecture on ballistics.

"Why me?" he asked, because the universe had a way of assigning improbable tasks to people who had once been good at memorizing Latin.

"You're cheap," Jahlain said bluntly, which was both a financial assessment and a character study. "And you have a medical background. That's useful for paperwork and plausible deniability. Also, you look like someone who can hold a clipboard without crying."

Jack took the envelope and felt the weight of it like a new kind of responsibility. He had imagined heroics in the form of saving lives; now heroics looked suspiciously like balancing a ledger and not getting caught.

"Remember the rules," Jahlain said, leaning in with the kind of conspiratorial whisper usually reserved for gossip about office birthday cakes. "Never break the code. Keep it clean. Keep it quiet. And for the love of all that is reasonable, don't call us on weekends unless it's an emergency or you've found a particularly good parking spot."

Jack nodded, because nodding is a universal language for "I understand" and "I will probably panic later." He left the office with the envelope in his pocket and a head full of conflicting advice: his medical oath, his father's range lessons, and Jahlain's pragmatic directives.

Outside, the south-side air felt cooler, as if the city itself were taking a breath. Jack walked away from the building and tried to imagine the next steps without picturing a montage of bad decisions set to dramatic music. He rehearsed his mantra—**Pay the bills. Keep hands clean. Never break the code**—and added a personal amendment: **If at all possible, avoid metaphors involving roofs.**

As he headed home, Jack realized that the world had a new rhythm: it was part clinic, part clandestine office, and entirely absurd. He had traded one kind of emergency for another, and somewhere between the potted plant and the manila envelope, he had discovered that life's most unexpected chapters often begin with a receptionist who wears sunglasses indoors and a nameplate that refuses to be ignored.

Chapter 3: Humble Beginnings

Jack had always thought surveillance would be glamorous: a trench coat, a fedora, and the kind of dramatic lighting that made even a parking lot look like a movie poster. Reality, as it turned out, involved a folding lawn chair, a thermos of coffee that tasted suspiciously like regret, and a playlist of podcasts about composting that he pretended to listen to so he wouldn't look like a man who spent his evenings watching other people's bad decisions.

For two months he became a part-time anthropologist of bad nightlife. He learned the rhythms of David Fordes's haunts the way a botanist learns a plant's seasons: where he wilted, where he bloomed, and where he was most likely to spill something sticky on the floor. Jack took notes in a little notebook that had once been used for lecture diagrams of the heart; now it contained doodles of bar stools and the occasional marginalia that read **"Do not become this man."**

David's preferred establishments were the kind of places that advertised "live music" and delivered something that sounded like a kazoo with an identity crisis. He frequented a dive where the jukebox was held together with optimism and duct tape, a convenience store that sold sandwiches with the same enthusiasm as expired milk, and a bar whose signature cocktail was called "Regret on the Rocks." Jack observed from a respectful distance, learning that David's gait could be described as "ambivalent," his laugh as "a little too loud for the room," and his decision-making as "consistently poor."

Jack's training in observation—years of reading vitals and noticing the tiny tells that separate a panic attack from indigestion—served him well. He could tell when David was about to leave a bar because he would suddenly become very interested in the menu, as if the menu held the answers to life's mysteries. He could tell when David was hiding out because he would start wearing a hat indoors and pretend to read a book he had no intention of finishing. Jack cataloged these behaviors like a collector of odd stamps, each one a clue.

And then, on a night that smelled of rain and bad decisions, Jack decided it was time to stop cataloging and start acting. He told himself he was being clinical about it—this was a case study, a final exam in a course he had not signed up for but was now enrolled in. He rehearsed his lines in the mirror: calm, efficient, not like someone who had once cried over a particularly moving episode of a medical drama. He practiced not looking like a man who had been watching another man's life for two months.

Breaking into David's apartment was, in Jack's mind, a cinematic affair. In reality it was a series of quiet, clumsy maneuvers that involved a coat hanger, a window that stuck, and the kind of breath-holding that made his chest feel like a balloon someone had forgotten to tie. He told himself the window was for ventilation and dramatic effect. The truth was less noble: it was the only way in without setting off an alarm that would have made the whole thing feel like a very public misunderstanding.

The apartment smelled like a thrift store that had given up on itself. There were magazines with headlines that promised reinvention and a couch that had clearly hosted more regrets than guests. Jack moved through the living room with the stealth of someone who had once performed a delicate procedure under fluorescent lights and now had to navigate a coffee table that seemed to have been designed by someone who hated symmetry.

There he was: David, slumped on the couch, a tragic figure in a cardigan that had seen better decades. For a moment Jack's brain tried to fit the scene into a textbook—pale, slack jaw, the kind of pallor that suggested the heart had simply decided to clock out. The clinical part of him whispered **"cardiac event."** The rest of him, the part that had been rehearsing a different ending, registered the absurdity of the timing.

Jack's first instinct was to check for a pulse, because old habits die harder than good intentions. The second instinct was to feel a wave of something that was not quite relief and not quite guilt—more like the sensation you get when you realize you've been rehearsing a joke and the punchline has already been delivered by someone else. He stood there, in the dim light, holding a flashlight like a prop in a very bad play.

Now, here's where Jack's moral compass did a little pirouette and then tried to sell tickets to the show. He had come prepared for a scenario that involved choices and consequences; he had not prepared for a scenario where the universe handed him a problem already solved. He had imagined confrontation, negotiation, maybe a dramatic monologue. Instead, he found a man who had been defeated by his own vices and the cruel arithmetic of a heart that had given up.

Jack did what any person with a questionable moral plan and a flair for dramatic closure might do: he panicked, he rationalized, and then he made a decision that would haunt his conscience and, if he were honest, make for a very awkward entry in his personal ledger. He performed the one action he had rehearsed in the privacy of his own head, the one that felt like a punctuation mark on a sentence he had been trying to end for weeks. He shot David in the head with his silenced 9mm.

There was little gore, no cinematic slow-motion. There was only the quiet, absurd finality of a choice made in a room that smelled faintly of stale beer and lost opportunities. Jack left the apartment the way he had entered it: awkwardly, with the grace of someone who had just tried to exit a stage and tripped over the curtain.

Outside, the rain had started in earnest, as if the weather itself wanted to wash away the evening's poor decisions. Jack walked away with his notebook in his pocket and a head full of thoughts that did not yet have names. He told himself stories to keep from thinking about the reality of what had happened: that sometimes life resolves itself, that sometimes you are merely a witness to the end of someone else's story, and that sometimes the universe has a sense of timing that is both cruel and inconvenient.

Back at his apartment, Jack made a list—because lists were how he organized chaos. **1. Pay bills. 2. Avoid moral collapse. 3. Learn to sleep without replaying the night.** He underlined the third item twice, because some lessons require emphasis.

He tried to laugh about it later, because humor is a useful anesthetic. He told himself the whole thing would make a good anecdote at a party he would never attend. He imagined telling his future grandchildren about the time he learned that life's punchlines are often improvised and rarely polite.

And so, with the rain still tapping a rhythm on the window and a city that had no interest in his internal monologue, Jack Nubold took his first step into a life that was less about saving people and more about surviving the consequences of choices that looked, in the light of day, like very bad ideas. He had started with humble intentions and ended with a story that would be difficult to tell without laughing and then immediately regretting the laugh.

Chapter 4: The Collection

Jack Nubold had never imagined that his first payday after medical school would involve descending into the basement of a mom-and-pop store that smelled like pickles, mothballs, and faintly, of despair. He had pictured white coats, sterile hallways, maybe a congratulatory handshake from a senior physician. Instead, he was greeted by a flickering fluorescent bulb and a sign taped to the door that read: **"Employees Only. Unless You're Here for Something Weird."**

The mom-and-pop store above was the kind of establishment that sold everything from canned peaches to socks with inspirational quotes. The owners were an elderly couple who seemed blissfully unaware that their basement doubled as the headquarters of a shadowy hitman accounting department. Jack passed them on his way in; the husband was arguing with a customer about whether pickled eggs counted as a vegetable, while the wife was knitting something that looked suspiciously like a balaclava.

Downstairs, the décor was less "family business" and more "Cold War bunker." A single desk sat in the middle of the room, covered in paperwork, a calculator the size of a microwave, and a small cactus that looked like it had seen things. Behind the desk sat Jahlain, the secretary of the hitman network, wearing her trademark sunglasses indoors and tapping away at a keyboard with the precision of someone who could probably file taxes blindfolded.

"Doctor Nubold," she said without looking up, her tone equal parts greeting and accusation. "You're here to collect."

Jack nodded, trying to look professional, though his idea of professionalism was still rooted in medical charts and not clandestine basements. "Yes. I, uh, completed the assignment."

Jahlain finally looked up, her expression somewhere between amusement and disdain. "I know. I watch the news. David Fordes, found dead. Heart attack, then a bullet to the head. Very tidy. Very… creative."

Jack shifted uncomfortably. "I didn't exactly plan the heart attack part. That was more of a… collaboration with fate."

Jahlain smirked. "Fate doesn't pay invoices. We do." She opened a drawer and pulled out a briefcase that looked like it had been borrowed from a spy movie. With a dramatic flourish, she clicked it open to reveal stacks of cash so neatly arranged they could have been used as props in a motivational seminar.

"One million dollars," she said, sliding the briefcase across the desk. "Untraceable. Spend it wisely. Or unwisely. We don't judge spending habits."

Jack stared at the money, his brain short-circuiting between relief, disbelief, and the sudden urge to buy a lifetime supply of ramen noodles just because he could. He reached out, touched the bills, and half-expected them to vanish like Monopoly money.

"And," Jahlain continued, pulling out a sleek black card that looked like it belonged in a dystopian credit commercial, "your hitman's credit account. Two hundred thousand dollars. Consider it a welcome bonus. You can use it for equipment, disguises, or, if you're feeling reckless, a very fancy espresso machine."

Jack blinked. "There's… a credit system?"

"Of course," Jahlain said, as if explaining gravity. "We're professionals. We have loyalty programs, reward points, even a newsletter. Don't look so surprised. You think assassins just Venmo each other?"

Jack laughed nervously, imagining a world where hitmen sent emojis with their payments. He tucked the card into his pocket, feeling both powerful and absurd.

"So," he said, trying to sound casual, "who's next?"

Jahlain leaned back in her chair, folding her hands like a chess master about to reveal a strategy. "That depends. You're still a novice. You've proven you can follow through, even if fate did half the work. But round two isn't something you rush into. When you're ready, you call us. Or we'll find you. Unless we need to find you."

Jack frowned. "That sounds… ominous."

"It's supposed to," Jahlain replied. "Keeps you on your toes. Also, it's in the handbook." She tapped a thick binder labeled **"Hitman Code: Revised Edition."**

Jack considered his options. He had the money, the credit, and the sudden realization that his life had taken a sharp left turn into absurdity. He thought about his medical oath, about saving lives, and then about the mountain of debt that had once seemed insurmountable. He thought about ramen noodles, too, because financial freedom made him hungry.

"I think I'll keep my head down," he said finally, trying to sound wise. "But I'll be around."

Jahlain raised an eyebrow. "That's what they all say. Then they call me two weeks later because they get bored and want another adrenaline rush. Or because they spent all their money on inflatable furniture. Either way, I'll be here."

Chapter 5: Let's Not, and Say We Did

Jack Nubold had never felt more like a responsible adult than the moment he logged into his student loan account and clicked **"Pay in Full."** The screen blinked, the balance dropped to zero, and a little animated confetti burst across the page. Jack stared at it like he had just cured cancer. He had spent years memorizing obscure medical terms, surviving caffeine overdoses, and stitching together patients who thought WebMD was a second opinion. And now, thanks to a briefcase full of untraceable cash from a secretary who worked in a basement that smelled like pickles, he was debt-free.

He leaned back in his chair, exhaled dramatically, and whispered to himself, "Jack Nubold, you magnificent genius. You did it. You're clean. You're methodical. No one knows. Man, I'm good."

He began pacing his apartment, which was decorated in the style of "recent graduate with questionable taste." The couch had a suspicious stain that looked like it had been there since the Carter administration, and the coffee table was held together with duct tape and optimism. Jack strutted back and forth like a man rehearsing for a TED Talk titled *How I Outsmarted Everyone and Paid Off My Loans in One Easy Step.*

He even practiced his acceptance speech in case anyone ever asked him how he did it. "Well," he said to the empty room, "I was disciplined. I was precise. I was like a surgeon with a scalpel, except the scalpel was a silenced pistol and the patient was already dead. But hey, details."

Jack was halfway through congratulating himself when his phone buzzed. He froze. The ringtone was a cheerful jingle that sounded wildly inappropriate for someone in his line of extracurricular work. He picked it up, cleared his throat, and answered with the kind of confidence that only comes from paying off six figures of debt.

"Hello, who is this?" Jack asked, trying to sound casual, like he was expecting a call from a pizza delivery guy.

The voice on the other end was female, calm, and unsettlingly polite. "I am a friend. If this is Jack, we found a flaw in your work. Wait for our arrival."

Jack blinked. His brain tried to process the words, but all it could come up with was, *Flaw? Arrival? Friend?* He looked around his apartment as if the furniture might explain things. The couch offered no answers. The duct-taped coffee table remained silent.

"Uh," Jack stammered, "I think you've got the wrong number. This is… uh… Jeff. Jeff Noodle. Totally different guy."

The voice didn't miss a beat. "Jack, we'll see you soon."

Click.

Jack stared at the phone like it had just insulted his mother. His heart did a small tap dance in his chest. He grabbed his backpack, stuffed it with essentials—wallet, toothbrush, a half-eaten granola bar—and muttered, "Nope. Nope, nope, nope. Not today."

He bolted out of the apartment, leaving behind the confetti-filled loan receipt on his laptop screen. The confetti continued to fall, mocking him with its cheerful celebration of financial responsibility.

Meanwhile, across town, Jahlain sat in her basement office beneath the mom-and-pop store, sipping tea and scrolling through news channels like a woman who had seen it all and judged it twice. The cactus on her desk leaned toward her as if it wanted to hear the gossip.

On the television, a coroner's report played. The anchor's voice was chipper, as if announcing the weather. "Months after the death of David Fordes, new findings reveal that the victim was already deceased before the gunshot wound occurred. Authorities are baffled."

Jahlain smirked, hung up her phone, and muttered, "Novices. Always think they're clever until the paperwork catches up." She adjusted her sunglasses, even though the basement lighting was dim enough to make sunglasses redundant, and scribbled a note in her ledger: **Jack Nubold—flaw detected.**

Back in his apartment building, Jack was sprinting down the hallway like a man who had just remembered he left the oven on. He passed his neighbor, Mrs. Henderson, who was carrying a basket of laundry. "Everything okay, dear?" she asked.

"Yep!" Jack shouted, fumbling with his backpack. "Just, uh, cardio. Doctor's orders. Gotta keep the heart rate up!"

Mrs. Henderson nodded approvingly. "Good boy. Don't forget to hydrate."

Jack barreled down the stairs, muttering to himself. "Flaw? What flaw? I was clean. I was methodical. I even wiped down the doorknob. Who checks for flaws in a dead guy? He was already dead! That's like grading a test after the student dropped out!"

He reached the street, looked both ways, and realized he had no plan. He had money, sure, but money didn't buy invisibility. He considered disguises: fake mustache, trench coat, maybe a wig. But he remembered his dad's advice from the shooting range: "Son, if you ever get in trouble, don't wear a wig. You'll just look like a guy in a wig."

Jack sighed. "Thanks, Dad."

He ducked into a diner, ordered a coffee, and tried to look inconspicuous. The waitress gave him a suspicious glance when he asked if they accepted untraceable currency. He quickly backtracked. "I mean, uh, regular money. Totally normal money. With presidents on it."

As he sipped his coffee, Jack realized the absurdity of his situation. He had gone from med school graduate to debt-free hitman to fugitive in less time than it took to microwave a burrito. He thought about calling Jahlain, but he suspected her advice would be something like, "Congratulations, you're doomed."

The television in the diner played the same coroner's report Jahlain had watched. Jack nearly spit out his coffee when he heard the anchor say, "The victim was dead before the bullet wound."

He slumped in his booth, muttering, "Let's not, and say we did. That's my new motto. Forget the game. Forget the code. Forget everything. I'm out. I'm retired. Effective immediately."

The waitress refilled his coffee and gave him a look. "You talking to yourself, honey?"

Jack smiled weakly. "Yep. Practicing speeches. For a TED Talk. Title: *How Not to Be a Hitman.*"

The waitress shrugged. "Sounds niche."

Jack nodded. "Yeah. But niche pays the bills. Or at least it used to."

And with that, Jack Nubold sat in a diner booth, sipping coffee, plotting his escape, and wondering how long it would take before "friends" arrived to discuss his flaw. He had paid his debts, but the universe had decided he still owed interest—in chaos, comedy, and consequences.

Chapter 6: What's It Worth to You

Jack Nubold arrived in Toronto the next day with the kind of paranoia usually reserved for people who Google their symptoms and convince themselves they have seventeen rare diseases. He checked into a hotel that advertised "luxury amenities" but delivered a bed that squeaked like a rusty accordion and a minibar stocked entirely with off-brand sodas. He paced the room, muttering to himself, "Wanted. I'm wanted. For something. I don't know what. But definitely something."

Meanwhile, in an undisclosed location that looked suspiciously like a basement office decorated by someone who hated joy, Jahlain sat at her desk. She was writing up a document with the intensity of a novelist who had just discovered deadlines. Her cactus leaned toward her, as if trying to read over her shoulder. The phone rang.

A male voice came through, sounding like he had swallowed gravel for breakfast. "We arrived. The body has moved."

Jahlain didn't flinch. She adjusted her sunglasses, even though the room was dim enough to make sunglasses a health hazard, and replied, "I've got this. Disperse." She hung up with the kind of authority that suggested she had once fired someone for misusing a paperclip.

Back at the hotel, Jack's phone buzzed. He answered cautiously, like a man expecting either a pizza delivery confirmation or a death threat.

"Jack," Jahlain's voice said, calm and efficient. "Read your target's list. It's been updated."

Jack blinked. "Updated? Like a software patch? Do I need to restart myself?"

"Just read it," Jahlain snapped, because patience was not her brand.

Jack dug out his tablet, which was covered in fingerprints and regret. He opened the list, half-expecting to see his own name highlighted in neon. To his relief, he wasn't on it. He exhaled dramatically, like a man who had just survived a pop quiz.

Then he saw it: **Mathan Anders.** His friend. The guy who had gotten him into this mess in the first place. The man who had once convinced him that "hitman work" was just another form of freelance consulting.

Jack groaned. "This can't be good."

He stared at the screen, trying to rationalize. Maybe it was a typo. Maybe they meant *Nathan Andrews,* a completely different person who just happened to have a similar name and equally bad life choices. But the list was clear, and Jack knew better than to argue with lists maintained by people who carried silencers as casually as pens.

The job description was short, blunt, and terrifyingly cheerful: **Target: Mathan Anders. Reward: $300,000. Bonus: $50,000 hitman's credit.**

Jack rubbed his temples. "Three hundred grand and fifty in credit. That's… that's a lot of ramen noodles. That's a new couch. That's… probably therapy bills, too."

He paced the hotel room, weighing his options. On one hand, Mathan was his friend, the guy who had once lent him twenty bucks for pizza and introduced him to the world of clandestine contracts. On the other hand, three hundred thousand dollars was enough to buy a lifetime supply of pizza, plus the therapy sessions required to process the guilt of betraying a friend.

Jack tried to imagine explaining it to Mathan. "Hey buddy, funny story. You're on a list. I'm supposed to, you know, *handle* you. But don't worry, I'll make it quick and professional. Also, thanks for the referral."

He shook his head. "Nope. That conversation doesn't end well."

Still, the numbers were persuasive. Jack had learned that in this business, morality was negotiable, but math was not. He thought about his debt-free status, his shiny new hitman's credit card, and the possibility of finally upgrading from duct-taped furniture.

Finally, he sighed and muttered, "Fine. I'll take the job. But I'm not happy about it. Well, I'm a little happy about the money. But mostly unhappy. With a side of conflicted."

He called Jahlain back. "I'll do it," he said, trying to sound confident.

"Good," Jahlain replied. "Remember, Jack: it's not about friendship. It's about business. And business pays better than friendship."

Jack hung up, stared at his squeaky hotel bed, and whispered, "What's it worth to you, Jack? Apparently three hundred grand and fifty in credit. That's what it's worth."

He flopped onto the bed, which squeaked in protest, and stared at the ceiling. He imagined Mathan's face, his laugh, his terrible advice. He imagined the pizza they'd shared, the nights they'd complained about professors, the moment Mathan had casually said, "Hey, you ever thought about being a hitman?"

Jack groaned. "I should've just said no. I should've just said, 'Let's not, and say we did.' But no, I had to say yes. And now I'm in Toronto, plotting against my own friend, and the bed squeaks every time I breathe."

He rolled over, grabbed his tablet again, and stared at the list. Mathan's name glowed like a neon sign in a bad diner. Jack muttered, "This is going to be awkward. Very awkward. But at least I'll be rich. Rich and awkward. That's a brand I can live with."

And so, with a sigh, Jack Nubold accepted his next assignment: betray his friend for cash and credit. It wasn't noble, it wasn't heroic, and it definitely wasn't in any medical ethics textbook. But it was profitable. And in Jack's world, profit had a way of rewriting the rules.

Chapter 7: After All This

Mathan Anders was in his kitchen, humming off-key to a song that didn't exist, while attempting to cook something that looked suspiciously like spaghetti but smelled like regret. He had three pots going at once, none of which seemed to contain anything edible. One pot was boiling water with no pasta, another was simmering tomato sauce that had the consistency of lava, and the third contained what might have been chicken or possibly a science experiment.

Just as Mathan was sprinkling oregano with the confidence of a man who had never read a recipe, there was a knock at the door. He wiped his hands on a towel that had once been white but now resembled a Jackson Pollock painting and opened it.

Jack Nubold stood there, looking like a man who had just discovered his name on a very unpleasant list. He didn't bother with pleasantries. "The hit isn't for you, Mathan. It's for me."

Mathan blinked. "What? But it has your name…"

Jack nodded grimly. "Exactly. Which is why I'm here. Because apparently, I'm the target."

Mathan sighed, ushered Jack inside, and gestured toward the bubbling chaos on the stove. "Sit down. Let me tell you how this works. Also, don't eat anything. I'm ninety percent sure this sauce is flammable."

Jack sat at the kitchen table, which was covered in mismatched placemats and a stack of unopened mail. Mathan leaned against the counter, adopting the tone of a man who had explained this sort of thing far too many times.

"See, Jack," Mathan began, "a low-level hit on someone you know is basically bait. It's designed to get you out in the open. Nobody takes those jobs seriously because they're too messy. So instead, they put your name on the list, knowing you'll panic and show up somewhere dumb— like here, in my kitchen, while I'm cooking what might be chicken but could also be a shoe."

Jack rubbed his temples. "So you're saying… I'm the target. Not you."

"Exactly," Mathan said, stirring the lava sauce with a spoon that looked like it had been through a war. "Why? I don't know. Maybe you annoyed someone. Maybe you paid off your loans too quickly and made the rest of us look bad. Maybe you just have one of those faces."

Jack groaned. "What do I do?"

Mathan shrugged. "You're the hitman. You can escape. Or you can fight to clear your name. Personally, I'd recommend escape. Fighting usually involves paperwork, and paperwork is worse than death."

Jack slumped in his chair, staring at the pile of unopened mail. "Escape sounds good. But where? How? I can't exactly book a flight under 'Jack Nubold, Professional Target.'"

Mathan pointed his spoon at him like a sage delivering wisdom. "Talk to Jahlain. She knows why. She's the secretary of secrets, the keeper of ledgers, the woman who can file your death certificate before you even sneeze. If anyone knows why you're on the list, it's her."

Jack frowned. "She can help me?"

Mathan smirked. "She can help you, sure. But remember— she can also get you killed. She's like a librarian who hands out books and occasionally throws them at your head. You never know which version you're going to get."

Jack stood up, pacing the kitchen. "So my options are: run, fight, or talk to Jahlain and risk being turned into paperwork."

"Pretty much," Mathan said, tasting his sauce and immediately regretting it. "You're in the game now, Jack. And the game doesn't care if you're a novice or a professional. It just wants you to dance."

Jack muttered, "I didn't sign up for dancing. I signed up for debt relief."

Mathan shrugged again, tossing a questionable piece of chicken into the trash. "Well, congratulations. You're debt-free and possibly doomed. That's balance, my friend."

Jack stopped pacing, looked at Mathan, and said, "You know, for someone who got me into this mess, you're awfully calm about me being the target."

Mathan grinned. "Calm? Jack, I'm making dinner that could kill me faster than any hitman. Perspective."

Jack sighed, grabbed his backpack, and headed for the door. "Fine. I'll talk to Jahlain. But if she tries to kill me, I'm blaming you."

Mathan raised his spoon in salute. "Fair enough. Just remember: she's the only one who knows why you're on the list. And if you survive, bring me back something edible. Preferably pizza."

Jack left the apartment, muttering under his breath. "Debt-free, doomed, and now I have to negotiate with a secretary who might file me under 'miscellaneous fatalities.' Perfect."

Back in the kitchen, Mathan tasted his sauce again, winced, and said to himself, "Yep. Definitely flammable."

Chapter 8: I Got Paid for This

Jack Nubold had never thought his life would involve secure phone lines, whispered threats, and debt collectors who carried silencers instead of clipboards. Yet here he was, sitting in a hotel room with a phone that looked like it had been stolen from a spy movie prop department, waiting for the inevitable call.

The line clicked, and Jahlain's voice came through, smooth and sharp, like someone who had spent years practicing how to sound both professional and terrifying.

"Jack," she said, "death is the only escape. But you can come in and talk about this."

Jack winced. "That's not exactly a motivational slogan. You might want to workshop that."

Jahlain ignored him. "We know you didn't complete your hit. David Fordes was already dead when you arrived. You took credit for it. You owe us… or do we owe you?"

Jack rubbed his temples. "Look, I want out. How about I do some complementary hits to pay you back? Like a buy-one-get-one-free situation. You know, a loyalty program."

There was a pause. Jack imagined Jahlain adjusting her sunglasses in a dim basement, rolling her eyes so hard they could power a small generator.

"The agency understands and accepts," she said finally. "Choose your targets. You owe us one million dollars… plus interest."

Jack muttered under his breath, "Crooks. Absolute crooks."

He hung up, grabbed his backpack, and wandered into a vacant office building that looked like it had been abandoned by accountants who couldn't handle the stress.

The place smelled faintly of dust and broken dreams. He found a desk, sat down, and pulled out his tablet.

The target list glowed on the screen, a digital menu of questionable morality. Jack scrolled through names like he was browsing Netflix, muttering commentary as he went.

"Too complicated. Too messy. Too much paperwork. Oh, this guy's allergic to shellfish—tempting, but too niche."

Finally, he stopped at a name: **Barry Kimbon.**

Barry was described as a "cook for hire," which sounded less like a criminal and more like someone who catered weddings. But the notes clarified: Barry had taken a casino for a lot of money. He was part chef, part con artist, and apparently very bad at blackjack.

Jack grinned. "Perfect. A cook who stole from a casino. That's practically poetic. And the payout is one-point-five million. That's enough to clear my debt, pay the interest, and maybe buy a couch that doesn't squeak every time I sit down."

He leaned back in his chair, laughing to himself. "I can do this hit and be home in time for breakfast. Easy. Piece of cake. Or piece of omelet, since he's a cook."

Jack imagined the scenario: Barry in a kitchen, flipping pancakes with the confidence of a man who thought he'd beaten the house. Jack sneaking in, silencer ready, like a culinary critic with very harsh reviews. He pictured himself walking out, pockets full of cash, stopping at a diner for celebratory waffles.

The absurdity of it all hit him. He was a doctor, trained to save lives, now plotting to take out a chef who had stolen from a casino. He chuckled. "I got paid for this. I actually got paid for this. Somewhere, my professors are crying into their anatomy textbooks."

He scrolled through Barry's profile again. The man had a reputation for flamboyant cooking and questionable ethics. His signature dish was something called "Roulette Risotto," which Jack assumed was just rice with random ingredients thrown in. Barry had apparently once catered a mob wedding and served soup so salty it nearly caused a riot.

Jack shook his head. "This guy deserves it just for the risotto."

He stood up, pacing the dusty office. "Okay, Jack. Focus. Step one: find Barry. Step two: make it look professional. Step three: collect one-point-five million, laugh all the way to the bank, and maybe finally buy decent furniture."

He sat back down, scribbling notes on a scrap of paper like he was planning a science experiment. "Variables: Barry's location, Barry's cooking schedule, Barry's gambling habits. Hypothesis: Barry will be easier to hit than a piñata at a children's party."

Jack laughed again, the sound echoing through the empty office. "I can't believe this is my life. I got paid for this. Paid to pretend I'm James Bond, except with student loans and questionable ethics."

He imagined calling his mother. "Hey Mom, guess what? I'm debt-free. Oh, how? Well, funny story. I took out a chef who stole from a casino. Don't worry, it was very professional. I even wore gloves."

He shook his head. "Nope. Definitely not telling Mom."

Jack closed his tablet, stuffed it back into his bag, and stood up with renewed confidence. "Barry Kimbon, you flamboyant risotto thief, your time is up. And I'll be home in time for breakfast."

He strutted out of the office building, humming, to himself, feeling like the star of a very low-budget action comedy. Somewhere in the distance, a pigeon cooed judgmentally, but Jack ignored it. He had a mission, a payout, and the absurd satisfaction of knowing that his career path now included phrases like "complementary hits" and "casino cook."

And as he walked into the night, Jack couldn't help but laugh. "I got paid for this. And I'm about to get paid again. Breakfast is on me."

Chapter 9: Shake a Leg, Jack

Jack Nubold had tracked Barry Kimbon for weeks, and the trail had led him to Omaha, Nebraska—a place Jack had never imagined would be the hideout of a casino-robbing cook. Omaha was supposed to be about steaks, cornfields, and polite Midwestern charm, not fugitive chefs with a taste for ill-gotten gains. But Barry was here, living his best life, and Jack was determined to put an end to it.

Barry was not hard to spot. He was portly, round in the way that suggested he had enjoyed his "upfall" far too much. Jack had expected a man on the run to be lean, paranoid, and constantly looking over his shoulder. Instead, Barry looked like he had just finished a buffet and was considering dessert. He waddled through town with the confidence of someone who believed hiding in Omaha was the equivalent of invisibility.

Jack followed him discreetly, jotting down notes like a detective who had accidentally wandered into a sitcom. Barry's routine was simple: eat, drink, gamble online, repeat. His favorite haunt was a bar that smelled faintly of stale beer and fried pickles. Jack learned Barry's home address, his favorite bartender's name, and even the fact that Barry tipped poorly. "Figures," Jack muttered. "Steal millions from a casino but stiff the guy who brings you nachos."

The night of the hit, Jack set up across the street from Barry's bar. He had chosen a rooftop vantage point, the kind of place action heroes always pick in movies. In reality, it was dark, hot, and smelled faintly of pigeon droppings. Jack lay prone with his silenced pistol, sweating through his shirt, muttering to himself about how glamorous this job wasn't.

Inside the bar, Barry was living his best life. He sat at the counter, phone in hand, scrolling through the news while sipping a drink that looked more like liquid sugar than alcohol. The television above the bar blared a local news segment: "And in tonight's top story, a swarm of locusts has descended on the area. Experts say it's seasonal, but residents are advised to stay indoors."

Barry laughed so hard he nearly spilled his drink. "Locusts! In Omaha! What's next, frogs falling from the sky?" He slapped the bar, amused at nature's sense of humor, and ordered another round.

Jack, meanwhile, adjusted his scope. He had Barry in his sights. The timing was perfect: Barry was drunk, distracted, and about to stumble out into the night. Jack steadied his breathing, remembering his father's lessons at the shooting range. "Patience, son. Focus. And don't let bugs distract you."

As if summoned by irony, the locust swarm arrived.

It started as a faint buzzing, like a distant lawnmower. Then it grew louder, thicker, until the air itself seemed to vibrate. Jack squinted, trying to ignore it, but suddenly the rooftop was engulfed in a biblical plague. Locusts swarmed around him, bouncing off his face, his arms, his weapon. One particularly ambitious locust flew straight into his eye.

Jack cursed, flailing like a man caught in a slapstick routine. He tried valiantly to clear his vision, swiping at the insect, blinking furiously, muttering, "This is not in the handbook. No one said anything about locusts!"

Barry, oblivious, stumbled out of the bar, humming to himself, phone still in hand. Jack tried to refocus, but the locust in his eye refused to budge. His scope was useless, his vision blurred, and his patience evaporated. He swatted at the swarm, looking less like a professional hitman and more like a man auditioning for interpretive dance.

Barry waddled down the street, chuckling at the absurdity of locust season, while Jack lay on the rooftop, defeated by insects. He finally threw up his hands. "Forget it. I'll try again tomorrow. Barry gets away tonight. Congratulations, Omaha, you win."

Jack packed up his gear, muttering under his breath. "I survived med school, debt collectors, and shady secretaries, but I'm undone by bugs. Locusts! Of all things. I should've brought goggles. Or bug spray. Or maybe a flamethrower."

As Barry disappeared into the night, Jack climbed down from the rooftop, brushing locusts off his clothes. He looked ridiculous, covered in wings and dust, like a man who had lost a fight with a salad. He sighed, trudging back to his temporary hideout.

"Shake a leg, Jack," he told himself. "Tomorrow's another day. And hopefully, fewer bugs."

Back at his hotel, Jack collapsed onto the squeaky bed, staring at the ceiling. He replayed the evening in his mind: the perfect setup, the perfect timing, ruined by a swarm of insects. He laughed bitterly. "I got paid for this. Paid to fight locusts instead of hitting targets. What a career."

Meanwhile, Barry was at home, blissfully unaware of how close he had come to disaster. He reheated leftovers, chuckled at the news again, and thought to himself, "Locusts are the best security system I've ever had."

Jack, however, knew the truth. The job wasn't over. Barry was still out there, still portly, still smug. And Jack would be back. Next time, he promised himself, he'd bring goggles. And maybe a fly swatter.

Chapter 10: That Little Bit, Was a Lot

Jack Nubold had learned to expect the unexpected, but even he wasn't prepared for what happened the next time he had Barry Kimbon in his sights.

It was a crisp evening in Omaha, the kind of night where the air smelled faintly of fried food and regret. Jack had set up on another rooftop, determined to redeem himself after the locust fiasco. He had his silenced pistol ready, his scope adjusted, and his nerves steady. Barry was waddling out of his favorite bar, phone in hand, scrolling through memes like a man who had no idea half the underworld wanted him gone.

Jack whispered to himself, "Okay, Barry. Tonight's the night. No bugs, no distractions, just clean and professional." He steadied his breathing, lined up the shot, and squeezed the trigger—

—but before he could fire, Barry dropped like a sack of potatoes.

Jack blinked. "Wait… what?"

Barry hadn't tripped. He hadn't fainted. He had been shot. By someone else.

Jack lowered his weapon, scanning the area. Somewhere in the shadows, another hitman had beaten him to the punch. Barry lay sprawled on the sidewalk, his phone still glowing with a meme about cats. Jack's jaw dropped. He was scared, amazed, and slightly offended.

"Seriously?" Jack muttered. "I spent weeks tracking this guy, sweating on rooftops, fighting locusts, and someone else just strolls in and takes him out? That's rude. That's downright unprofessional."

He sat back, shaking his head. Of course Barry was a high-value target. Of course multiple hitmen were after him. Jack should have figured this much. Barry wasn't just a cook who stole from a casino; he was practically a walking jackpot.

Jack thought back to his first job, the one that had gotten him into this mess. He remembered David Fordes, already dead when Jack arrived, and how he had foolishly taken credit for it. That little bit of dishonesty had snowballed into debt, suspicion, and a career path that now involved rooftops and bug swarms. He wasn't going to make the same mistake twice.

"Nope," Jack said firmly, packing up his gear. "Not this time. I'm not claiming someone else's work. That's how you end up on the wrong side of the list. And I've already got enough problems."

He stuffed his pistol back into his bag, folded up his scope, and trudged down the fire escape. Barry's body was already attracting attention, and Jack had no interest in explaining why he was lurking on a rooftop with a silencer.

Back at his hideout, Jack pulled out his Hitman phone—a sleek, ominous device that looked like it had been designed by someone who hated joy. He checked his messages, hoping for a reprieve, maybe even a "Good job, Jack!" from Jahlain. Instead, the screen lit up with a single message:

"Time is ticking and your dinner is ready."

Jack frowned. "Dinner? I didn't order takeout. Unless this is code for… oh no."

He opened the app, and sure enough, the message referred to a new hit list update. The agency had a flair for cryptic metaphors, and apparently "dinner" meant "fresh targets." Jack sighed, scrolling through the list like a man browsing a menu he couldn't afford.

The names glowed on the screen, each one a potential payday, each one a potential disaster. Jack knew the rules: he owed the agency money, and the only way to pay it back was through successful hits. But he also knew the darker truth—if he didn't cover his debt soon, his own name would appear on the list.

He imagined it: **Jack Nubold, novice hitman, debt delinquent. Reward: one million dollars. Bonus: bragging rights.**

Jack shuddered. "Nope. Not happening. I am not going to be the entrée on someone else's dinner menu."

He scrolled through the list, muttering commentary like a man reviewing Yelp. "Too complicated. Too far away. Too many bodyguards. Oh, this guy's allergic to peanuts—tempting, but too messy."

Finally, he leaned back, rubbing his temples. The pressure was mounting. He had dodged locusts, lost Barry to another hitman, and now the clock was ticking. The agency didn't care about excuses. They cared about results. And if Jack didn't deliver soon, he'd be the next headline.

He paced his apartment, muttering to himself. "Okay, Jack. Focus. You need a target. You need a plan. And you need to not die. That's the trifecta. Easy, right? Totally easy."

His phone buzzed again, another reminder from the agency:

"Don't let dessert be you."

Jack groaned. "They really need to stop with the food metaphors. I'm starving and terrified at the same time."

He sat down, staring at the glowing list. Each name was a chance to clear his debt, but each name was also a step deeper into the absurd world he had stumbled into. He thought about his medical degree, his professors, his oath to save lives. Then he thought about his bills, his debt, and the million-dollar bounty that had once seemed like salvation.

Jack sighed, muttering to himself. "That little bit was a lot. One tiny mistake, one dead guy I didn't actually kill, and now I'm stuck in this circus. I should've just opened a clinic. Or sold artisanal bandages online. Anything but this."

He closed his phone, flopped onto his squeaky couch, and stared at the ceiling. Tomorrow, he'd pick a target. Tomorrow, he'd try again. But tonight, he was just a debt-ridden doctor-turned-hitman, wondering how his life had turned into a comedy of errors.

And somewhere, in the shadows, another hitman was probably laughing at him.

Chapter 11: Next Pick, Might Be It

Jack Nubold had finally decided that his next target needed to be something clean, simple, and—most importantly—low drama. After weeks of chasing chefs, dodging locusts, and nearly being outdone by other hitmen, he was tired of theatrics. He wanted a job that didn't involve rooftop sweating, biblical plagues, or existential crises.

So he did his homework. Jack sat at his desk with his tablet glowing like a sinister menu, scrolling through the updated hit list. He treated it like online shopping: "Too expensive. Too complicated. Too many bodyguards. Oh, this one looks like it comes with free shipping." He wanted someone so unappealing as a target that no other hitman would bother. The kind of person whose name on the list would make professionals groan and say, "Pass."

Finally, he found him. A man so boring, so utterly forgettable, that Jack almost fell asleep reading his profile. The notes described him as "low-value, low-risk, low-interest." He lived alone, had no friends, no enemies worth mentioning, and his hobbies included stamp collecting and complaining about the weather. Jack grinned. "Perfect. Nobody wants this guy. He's the clearance rack of targets."

Jack leaned back in his chair, satisfied. "This is it. Closed and shut case. All I have to do is show up. No drama, no locusts, no rival hitmen swooping in at the last second. Just me, my checklist, and a payday."

But Jack wasn't going to do it alone. He called his friend Mathan Anders, the man who had gotten him into this mess in the first place. Mathan answered on the second ring, sounding like he was in the middle of burning dinner again.

"Jacko!" Mathan said cheerfully. "What's up? You sound like a man who's about to make a questionable life choice."

Jack explained the situation. "I've got a target. Easy pick. Nobody wants him. It's practically a freebie. I'll supply the intel, you handle the actual… you know… logistics."

Mathan chuckled. "So you want me to do the heavy lifting while you play lookout?"

"Exactly," Jack said. "I'll keep an eye out for other hitmen. You do the kill. Teamwork makes the dream work."

Mathan agreed, mostly because he loved the thrill of it and partly because he owed Jack for years of bad advice. Together, they planned the operation with the precision of two men who had watched too many crime dramas and thought they could wing it.

The target lived in a small, unimpressive house on the edge of town. Jack described it as "the kind of place where dreams go to die quietly." Mathan prepared his gear, while Jack packed snacks for the stakeout. "You never know how long these things take," Jack said, stuffing granola bars into his bag. "And I don't want to get hangry while watching you work."

On the night of the hit, Jack stationed himself across the street, binoculars in hand, looking like a man auditioning for the role of "Suspicious Neighbor." Mathan slipped inside the house with the grace of someone who had once practiced break-ins on his own garage.

Jack scanned the area, muttering to himself. "Okay, no rival hitmen. No cops. No nosy neighbors. Just me, Mathan, and Mr. Forgettable inside." He felt oddly proud of himself. For once, things were going smoothly.

Inside, Mathan did his part quickly and efficiently. The target barely noticed what was happening, which was fitting for a man whose entire existence had been defined by being overlooked. Mathan emerged minutes later, wiping his hands like he had just finished a particularly messy sandwich.

"All done," Mathan said casually.

Jack blinked. "That's it? No drama? No chase? No swarm of insects?"

"Closed and shut case," Mathan replied. "You picked the right guy. Honestly, I think he was relieved."

Jack laughed, shaking his head. "I can't believe it. We actually pulled off a hit without chaos. This feels… wrong. Like we're cheating."

They packed up their gear and walked away, blending into the night like two men who had just finished a very strange group project. Jack kept glancing over his shoulder, half-expecting something ridiculous to happen—a rival hitman popping out of a bush, a meteor crashing down, or the target suddenly resurrecting to complain about the weather one last time. But nothing happened.

Back at their hideout, Jack checked his phone. The agency had already updated his account: one successful hit, debt reduced, credit increased. He stared at the numbers, grinning. "Mathan, we did it. We're actually ahead. I might not end up on the list after all."

Mathan raised an eyebrow. "Don't get cocky. This was a fluke. Next time, you'll probably end up chasing a circus clown through a cornfield."

Jack shrugged. "Maybe. But for now, I'm going to enjoy this moment. Clean, simple, profitable. Next pick might be it—the one that gets me out of debt for good."

He leaned back, munching on a granola bar, savoring the rare taste of victory. For once, Jack wasn't sweating, panicking, or swatting bugs out of his eyes. He was just a debt-ridden doctor-turned-hitman, finally feeling like he had chosen wisely.

Of course, deep down, Jack knew the universe had a sense of humor. And it was only a matter of time before his next "easy" job turned into another comedy of errors. But tonight, he let himself believe.

"Next pick might be it," Jack said aloud, smiling. "And if it isn't, well… at least I've got snacks."

Chapter 12: Out of the Grave I Go

Jack Nubold had finally done it. He had made a kill, collected his payout, and for the first time in months, he felt like he could breathe without hearing the faint sound of debt collectors sharpening their knives in the background. He strutted down the street like a man who had just solved all his problems with one decisive action. His shoulders were back, his chin was high, and his inner monologue was practically singing: *"Debt-free, baby! Out of the grave I go!"*

It was a glorious moment. Jack imagined himself as a phoenix rising from the ashes, except instead of wings he had a squeaky leather jacket, and instead of fire he had a silenced pistol tucked in his bag. He even practiced a victory speech in his head: "Ladies and gentlemen, I am proud to announce that I am no longer a walking IOU. I am now a free man, a professional, a legend in the making."

But Jack's life had a habit of turning victory laps into pratfalls.

Because little did Jack know, his "pick of the litter" target was not the clean, simple case he thought it was. No, this one came with fine print. And Jack, being Jack, had not read the fine print.

The agency had rules—rules Jack barely understood and rarely followed. One of those rules was that every kill had to be clean, tidy, and indisputable. No loose ends, no sloppy work, no "oops, I think he was already dead" situations. Jack's first kill had been a disaster, and though he thought he had redeemed himself with this one, the truth was that he had simply traded one debt for another.

As Jack strutted into his apartment, humming a triumphant tune, his Hitman phone buzzed. He pulled it out, expecting a congratulatory message, maybe even a digital confetti animation. Instead, the screen displayed a single line:

"Debt cleared? Think again."

Jack blinked. "Wait… what?" He tapped the screen, hoping it was a glitch. The phone buzzed again, this time with a longer message:

"Your latest kill was sloppy. You owe us. Again. Interest applies."

Jack's jaw dropped. "Sloppy? Sloppy?! I was meticulous! I even wore gloves!" He paced his apartment, waving the phone around like it was a misbehaving child. "I paid back my debt! I'm free! I'm out of the grave! You can't just bury me again!"

But the agency didn't care about Jack's theatrics. They cared about precision, and Jack's kill had apparently been less "precision" and more "enthusiastic improvisation."

Jack flopped onto his couch, which squeaked in protest, and groaned. "This is my life now. I claw my way out of the grave, and they shove me right back in. It's like financial whack-a-mole, but with corpses."

He replayed the kill in his mind, trying to figure out what had gone wrong. He had tracked the target, planned the timing, executed the shot. Sure, maybe he had left a few fingerprints on the doorknob. And maybe the neighbor's cat had seen him. And maybe he had celebrated a little too loudly afterward. But still—wasn't the point that the guy was dead?

Jack muttered to himself, "I swear, these people are crooks. Absolute crooks. They're like loan sharks, but with better stationery."

The phone buzzed again. **"You still have a debt to pay. Choose wisely."**

Jack threw his hands in the air. "Choose wisely? I can't even choose a decent couch! How am I supposed to choose another target?"

He paced the room, muttering like a man rehearsing for a comedy routine. "Out of the grave I go, they said. Debt-free, they said. And now? Back in the grave. Debt-full. I'm basically a zombie hitman. I rise, I fall, I owe, I pay. Rinse and repeat."

Jack imagined himself explaining this to Mathan. "Hey buddy, funny story. I killed a guy, paid off my debt, and now I owe more because apparently I wasn't clean enough. It's like paying off a credit card and then realizing you forgot the annual fee."

He sighed, collapsing back onto the couch. "This is my first real kill, and I already messed it up. Figures. I should've just stuck to medicine. At least when you mess up there, you can blame the insurance company."

Jack's phone buzzed one last time, delivering the final blow:

"Debt: $1,000,000. Interest: ongoing. Out of the grave? Not yet."

Jack stared at the screen, defeated. "One million dollars. Again. It's like they're recycling my debt. I'm basically on a subscription plan for failure."

He laughed bitterly, shaking his head. "Well, have at it, Jack. You still have a debt to pay. Out of the grave you go, right back into the hole. Congratulations, you're the world's least successful hitman."

But even as he sulked, Jack felt a flicker of determination. He wasn't going to let the agency bury him forever. He would find another target, plan another hit, and this time he would be clean. No sloppy fingerprints, no nosy cats, no rival hitmen swooping in at the last second. He would rise again, debt-free, triumphant.

He stood up, clenched his fists, and declared to the empty room: "Out of the grave I go! And this time, I'm staying out!"

The couch squeaked in response, as if mocking him.

Jack sighed. "Okay, maybe not staying out. But at least I'll try."

And with that, Jack Nubold, debt-ridden doctor-turned-hitman, prepared himself for the next round of absurdity. Because in his world, every victory was temporary, every debt was eternal, and every grave had a revolving door.

Acknowledgements:

I want to thank all the readers and digesters of written, and spoken, words, and of my stories. I also want to thank my family extended and associated.

Author's Note:

To you,

As this is a fictional story, I write this to acknowledge the

lives we live and the will to do what we need to do to

succeed as people.

Thank you,